I dedicate my part of this book
——————— to ———————
Rosemary Wells
in return for the great pleasure
she has given me
with her part of the book

IONA OPIE

——————— For ———————
Rosemary Sandberg

ROSEMARY WELLS

MY VERY FIRST MOTHER GOOSE

Edited by
IONA OPIE

Illustrated by
ROSEMARY WELLS

WALKER BOOKS
AND SUBSIDIARIES
LONDON • BOSTON • SYDNEY

MOTHER GOOSE,

that kind and quizzical old lady, knows all about human nature. For centuries she has been gathering rhymes that will help people along the bumpy road of life. "If they fall down," she says, "it is only to be expected – Jack and Jill fell down too." I imagine her sitting beside a large sack full of glistening versicles: "A two-year-old in a temper? 'Davy Davy Dumpling' would be just the thing"; "A grizzling three-year-old, on a rainy afternoon? I recommend a dance or two – 'Sally go round the sun' perhaps, with 'Shoo fly' to follow." What treasures she has! Places to go to, and places to come back to; "Over the hills and far away", then home to tea by the fireside, with a welcome of "Three good wishes" and "Three good kisses". Remedies for people who do not want to go to bed – "Up the wooden hill to Blanket Fair"; and for people who do not want to get up – "Elsie Marley's grown so fine". Jollifications that cheer parents as well as children, like "Dance to your daddy" and "Hi! hi! says Anthony".

There they lie, the nursery rhymes, so much at the back of our minds that we can't remember when we first learnt them. What did they give us, so long ago? A suggestion that mishaps might be funny rather than tragic, that tantrums can be comical as well as frightening, and that laughter is the cure for practically everything.

We seem to be born, too, with a love for music and the music of words (try singing "Boys and girls come out to play" to a baby of three months old). But introductions must be made. The words one first meets in nursery rhymes will always have a special magic, all the stronger for being mysterious and incomprehensible; and what pleasanter way to learn your numbers than through the black sheep's allocation of his bags of wool, or the enumeration of Mrs Hen's diversely-coloured chickens.

I firmly believe that Rosemary Wells is Mother Goose's second cousin, and has inherited the family point of view. Her illustrations exactly reflect Mother Goose's many moods: glumpish, her animals look wickedly askance at the world; happy, they almost dance off the page; cosily at home, there is no greater depth of content-ment. They make me shout with glee. She has learnt the family secrets, too. Even I had never heard the full story of "Cobbler, cobbler, mend my shoe", or knew that when the mouse ran down the clock, the cat was close by, asleep in his armchair.

Mother Goose will show newcomers to this world how astonishing, beautiful, capricious, dancy, eccentric, funny, goluptious, haphazard, intertwingled, joyous, kindly, loving, melodious, naughty, outrageous, pomsidillious, querimonious, romantic, silly, tremendous, unexpected, vertiginous, wonderful, x-citing, yo-heave-ho-ish and zany it is. And when we come to be grandmothers it is just as well to be reminded of these twenty-six attributes.

Iona Opie

Jerry Hall,

He is so small,

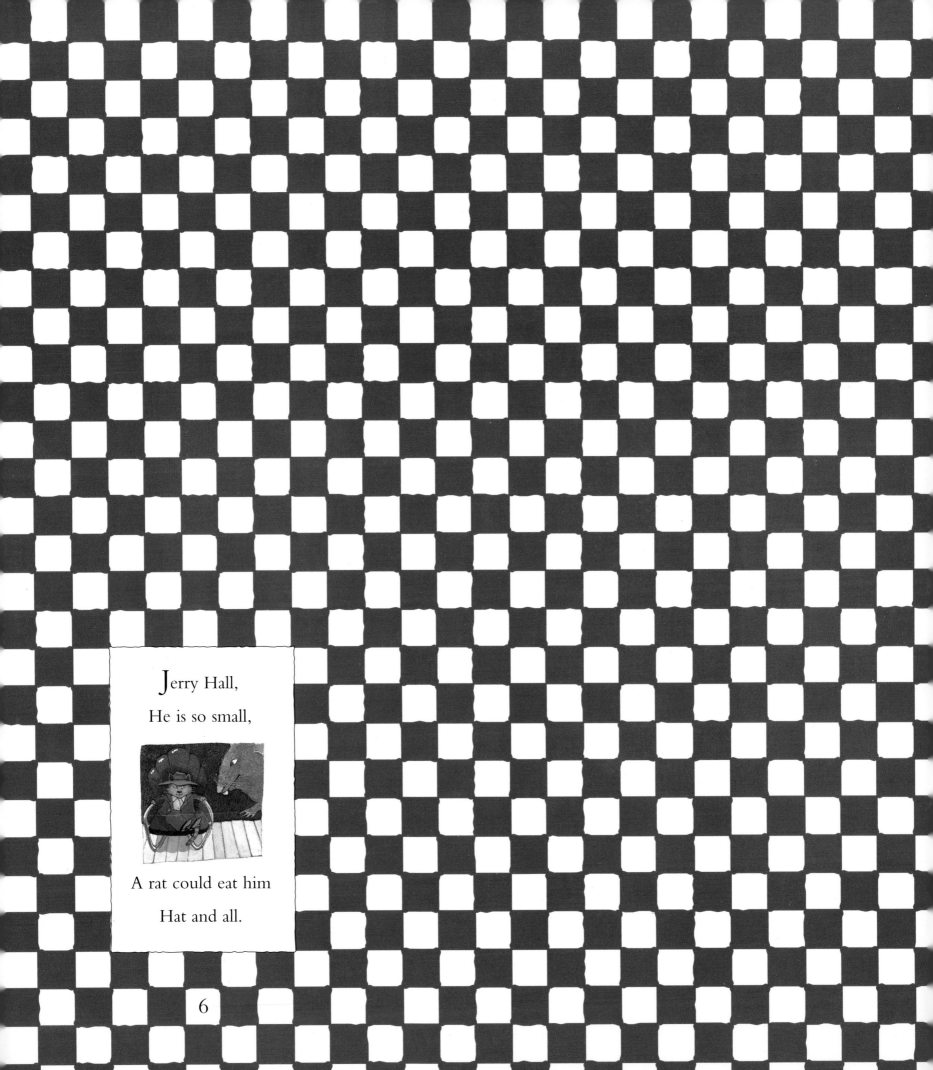

A rat could eat him

Hat and all.

Contents

Tom he was a piper's son,

He learned to play

  when he was young,

But all the tunes

  that he could play

Was, 'Over the hills

  and far away'.

Over the hills

  and a great way off,

The wind shall blow

  my top-knot off.

8

Chapter One
Jack and Jill

Jack and Jill went up the hill,
To fetch a pail of water;

Jack fell down and broke his crown,
And Jill came tumbling after.

Shoo fly, don't bother me,
Shoo fly, don't bother me,

Shoo fly, don't bother me,
I belong to somebody.

Boys and girls
  come out to play,
The moon doth shine
  as bright as day.
Leave your supper
  and leave your sleep,
And join your playfellows
  in the street.

Come with a whoop,
  and come with a call,
Come with a good will
  or not at all.
Up the ladder
  and down the wall,
A tuppenny loaf
  will serve us all.
You bring milk
  and I'll bring flour,
And we'll have a pudding
  in half an hour.

Humpty Dumpty sat on a wall,

Humpty Dumpty had a great fall.

All the king's horses and all the king's men

Couldn't put Humpty together again.

Down at the station, early in the morning,

See the little puffer-billies all in a row;

See the engine-driver pull his little lever –

Puff puff, peep peep, off we go!

Baa, baa, black sheep,

have you any wool?

Yes, sir, yes, sir,

three bags full.

One for the master,
  and one for the dame,
And one for the little boy
  who lives down the lane.

Cackle, cackle, Mother Goose,
Have you any feathers loose?

20

Truly have I, pretty fellow,
Quite enough to fill a pillow.

Little Boy Blue,
come blow your horn,

The sheep's
  in the meadow,
The cow's
  in the corn.

Where is the boy
  who looks after the sheep?
He's under a haycock
  fast asleep.

Will you wake him?
  No, not I,
For if I do,
  he's sure to cry.

23

To market, to market, to buy a fat pig,
Home again, home again, jiggety-jig.

To market, to market, to buy a fat hog,
Home again, home again, jiggety-jog.

Wash the dishes,
Wipe the dishes,
Ring the bell for tea;

Three good wishes,
Three good kisses,
I will give to thee.

Rain
on the
green
grass,

And
rain
on the
tree;

Rain
on the
house
top,

But not on me.

Warm hands, warm,
The men are gone to plough,
If you want to warm your hands,
Warm your hands now.

Ride a cock-horse to Banbury Cross
  To see a fine lady on a white horse;
    Rings on her fingers and bells on her toes,
      She shall have music wherever she goes.

Trot, trot, to Boston; trot, trot, to Lynn;
  Trot, trot, to Salem; home, home, again.

Horsie, horsie, don't you stop,
Just let your feet go clipetty clop;
Your tail goes swish, and the wheels go round –
Giddy up, you're homeward bound!

Father and Mother
and Uncle John,
Went to market one by one;
Father fell off – !
And Mother fell off – !

But Uncle John –
Went on, and on,
and on, and on—

and on, and on, and on...

Chapter Two
Hey Diddle, Diddle

Hey diddle, diddle,

the cat and the fiddle,

The cow jumped over the moon;

The little dog laughed

to see such fun,

And the dish ran away

with the spoon.

Sing a song of sixpence,
A pocket full of rye;
Four and twenty blackbirds
Baked in a pie.
When the pie was opened,
The birds began to sing;
Wasn't that a dainty dish
To set before the king?

Smiling girls, rosy boys,
Come and buy my little toys:
Monkeys made
    of gingerbread
And sugar horses
    painted red.

Handy spandy,
    sugary candy,
French almond rock;
    Bread and butter
    for your supper,
        That is all your
            mother's got.

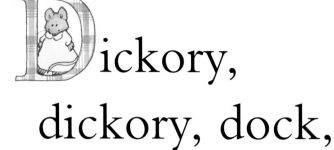Dickory,
dickory, dock,

The mouse ran
up the clock.

The clock struck one,
The mouse ran down,

Dickory,
dickory, dock.

Dickory,
dickory, dare,

The pig flew up
in the air.

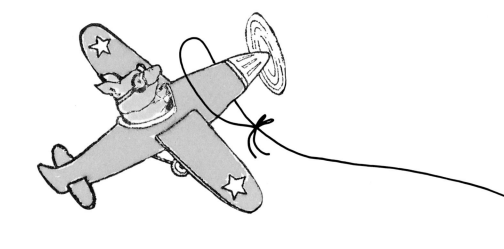

The man in brown
Soon brought him down,

Dickory,
dickory, dare.

There was a crooked man,

And he walked a crooked mile,

He found a crooked sixpence

Against a crooked stile.

He bought a crooked cat,

Which caught a crooked mouse,

And they all lived together

In a little crooked house.

42

The cock's on the house-top, blowing his horn;

The bull's in the barn, a-threshing the corn;

The maids in the meadow are making the hay;

The ducks in the river are swimming away.

Bat, bat,

Come under my hat,

And I'll give you a slice of bacon;

And when I bake, I'll give you a cake,

If I am not mistaken.

Great A, little a, bouncing B,
The Cat's in the cupboard

And can't see me.

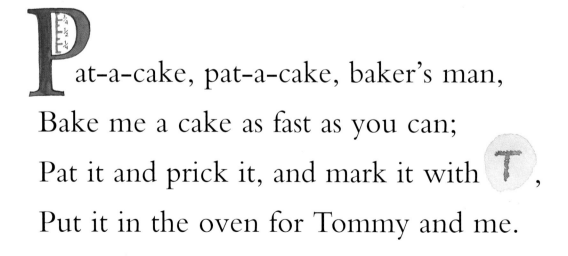

Pat-a-cake, pat-a-cake, baker's man,

Bake me a cake as fast as you can;

Pat it and prick it, and mark it with T,

Put it in the oven for Tommy and me.

Davy Davy Dumpling,
Boil him in a pot;
Sugar him and butter him,
And eat him while he's hot.

Little Jack Horner sat in a corner,

Eating his Christmas pie;

He put in his thumb, and pulled out a plum,

And said, What a good boy am I!

Hi! hi! says Anthony,
Puss is in the pantry,
Gnawing, gnawing,
A mutton mutton-bone;

See how she tumbles it,
See how she mumbles it,
See how she tosses
The mutton mutton-bone.

Sing, sing,
What shall I sing?
The cat's run away
With the pudding string!

Do, do,
What shall I do?
The cat's run away
With the pudding too!

Hickety, pickety, my black hen,

She lays eggs for gentlemen;

Gentlemen come every day

To see what my black hen doth lay.

Elsie Marley's grown so fine,

She won't get up to feed the swine,

But lies in bed till eight or nine.

Lazy Elsie Marley.

Pussy-cat, pussy-cat, where have you been?
I've been to London to look at the queen.

Pussy-cat, pussy-cat, what did you there?

I frightened a little mouse under her chair.

53

Dance to your daddy, You shall have a fishy
My little babby, In a little dishy,
Dance to your daddy, You shall have a fishy
My little lamb. When the boat comes in.

Puss came dancing
  out of a barn
With a pair of bagpipes
  under her arm;

She could sing nothing
  but 'Fiddle cum fee,
The mouse has married
  the bumblebee—'

Pipe, cat!

Dance, mouse!

We'll have a wedding

at our good house.

Chapter Three
Little Jumping Joan

Here am I, Little Jumping Joan;
When nobody's with me, I'm all alone.

I had a little nut tree, nothing would it bear
But a silver nutmeg and a golden pear.

The king of Spain's daughter came to visit me,
And all for the sake of my little nut tree.

I skipped over water, I danced over sea,
And all the birds in the air couldn't catch me.

Up the wooden hill to Blanket Fair,

What shall we have when we get there?

A bucket full of water

And a pennyworth of hay,

Gee up, Dobbin,

All the way!

If I had a donkey
that wouldn't go,

D'you think I'd beat him?
Oh, no, no.

I'd put him in a barn
and give him some corn,

The best little donkey
that ever was born.

From **Wibbleton** to **Wobbleton** is fifteen miles,

From **Wobbleton** to **Wibbleton** is fifteen miles,

From **Wibbleton** to **Wobbleton**, from **Wobbleton** to **Wibbleton**,

From **Wibbleton** to **Wobbleton** is fifteen miles.

Cobbler, cobbler, mend my shoe,

Get it done by half-past two;

Half-past two is much too late,

Get it done by half-past eight.

Stitch it up and stitch it down,

Then I'll give you half a crown.

One, two, three, four,

Mary's at the cottage door,

Five, six, seven, eight,

Eating cherries off a plate.

 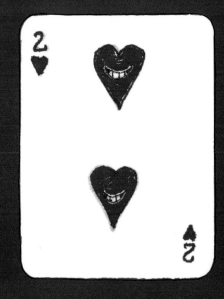  

One
for
sorrow

Two
for
joy

Three
for a
girl

Four
for a
boy

  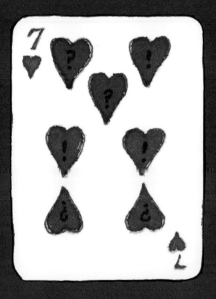 

Five
for
silver

Six
for
gold

Seven
for a
secret

Ne'er
to be
told.

Whose little pigs are these, these, these?
Whose little pigs
are these?

They are Roger the Cook's,
I know by their looks –
I found them among my peas.

Oh, the brave old duke of York,
He had ten thousand men;
He marched them up to the top of the hill,
And he marched them down again.
And when they were up, they were up,
And when they were down, they were down,
And when they were only half way up,
They were neither up nor down.

rs Mason

bought a basin;

Mrs Tyson said,

What a nice 'un;

What did it cost?

said Mrs Frost;

Half a crown,

said Mrs Brown;

Did it indeed?

said Mrs Reed;

It did for certain,

said Mrs Burton—

Then

Mrs Nix

up to her

tricks

Threw the

basin on the

bricks.

Half a pound of tuppenny rice,
Half a pound of treacle,
Mix it up and make it nice-
Pop goes the weasel!!

Ms. Greta Grizzly
Beartown
USA
50194

A penny for a spool of thread,
A penny for a needle,
That's the way the money goes—
Pop goes the weasel!

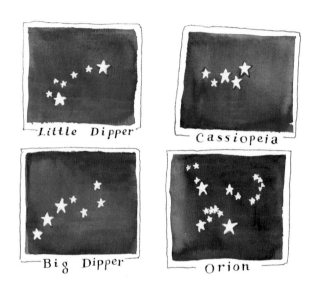

Little Dipper   Cassiopeia

Big Dipper   Orion

Star light, star bright,
First star I see tonight,
I wish I may, I wish I might,
Have the wish I wish tonight.

Sally go round the sun, Sally go round the moon, Sally go round the chimney pots on a Sunday afternoon.

Chapter Four

The Moon Sees Me

I see the moon,
And the moon sees me;

God bless the moon,
And God bless me.

The wind, the wind, the wind blows high,
The rain comes scattering down the sky.

She is handsome, she is pretty,
She is the girl of the golden city.
She goes a-courting, one, two, three,
Please and tell me who is she.

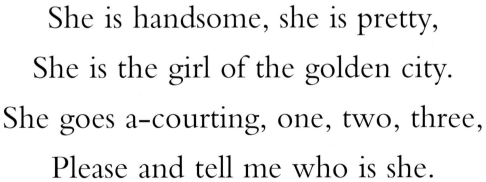

Blow, wind, blow!

And go, mill, go!

That the miller
may grind
his corn;
That the baker
may take it,
And into bread
make it,

And bring us a loaf
in the morn.

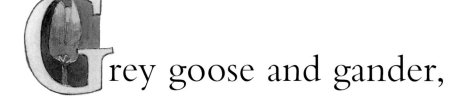rey goose and gander,

Waft your wings together,

And carry the good king's daughter

Over the one-strand river.

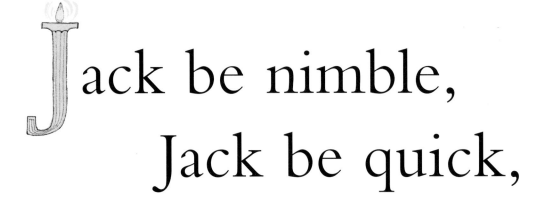Jack be nimble,
Jack be quick,

Jack jump over
The candlestick.

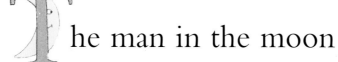he man in the moon

Came down too soon,

And asked his way

to Norwich;

He went by the south

And burnt his mouth

With supping cold

plum porridge.

Milkman, milkman,

where have you been?

In Buttermilk Channel up to my chin.

I spilt my milk, and I spoiled my clothes,

And I got a long icicle hung from my nose.

Polly put the kettle on,

Polly put the kettle on,

Polly put the kettle on,

We'll all have tea.

94

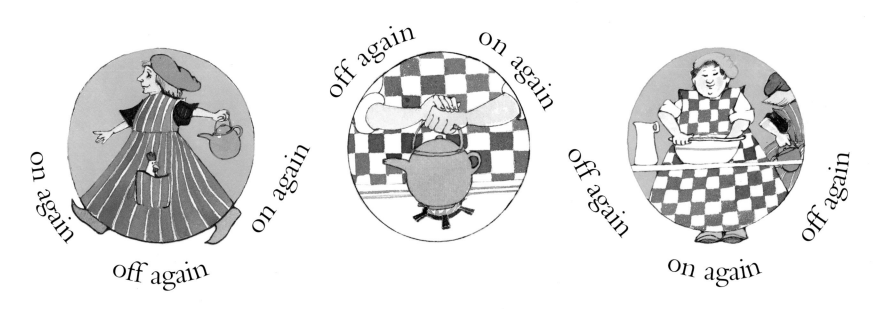

on again off again on again off again on again off again off again on again

Sukey take it off again,

Sukey take it off again,

Sukey take it off again,

They've all gone away.

I'll buy you a tartan bonnet,
And feathers to put upon it,

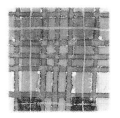

Buchanan

MacLeod

Stewart

McNeill

With a hush-a-bye and a lullaby
Because you are so like your daddy.

Wee Willie Winkie

runs

through

the town,

Upstairs and

downstairs

in his

night-gown,

Rapping at the window,

crying through the lock,

Are the children all in bed,

for now it's eight o'clock?

Matthew, Mark, Luke, and John,

Bless the bed that I lie on.

Four angels round my bed;

Two of them stand at my head,

Two of them stand at my feet,

All will watch me while I sleep.

The big ship

sails on

the alley

alley oh,

The alley

alley oh,

the alley

alley oh;

The big ship
sails on
the alley
alley oh,
On the last
day of
September.

How many miles to Babylon?
Three-score and ten.
Can I get there by candle-light?
Yes, and back again.

Open your gates as wide as the sky
And let the king and his men pass by.

Matthew, Mark, Luke, and John,
    Hold my horse till I leap on;
Hold him steady, hold him sure,
    And I'll get over the misty moor.

The mole

Lives in a hole;

He is blind –

I don't mind.

INDEX OF FIRST LINES

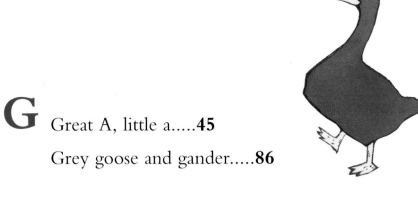

The mole

Lives in a hole;

He is blind –

I don't mind.

105

INDEX OF FIRST LINES

First published 1996 by Walker Books Ltd
87 Vauxhall Walk, London SE11 5HJ

6 8 10 9 8 7 5

This selection © 1996 Iona Opie
Illustrations © 1996 Rosemary Wells

This book has been typeset in M Bembo.

Printed in Hong Kong

British Library Cataloguing in
Publication Data
A catalogue record for this book is available
from the British Library.

ISBN 0-7445-4400-9

For

Diana Mann, because.

IONA OPIE

For

Amelia and Amy.

ROSEMARY WELLS

HERE COMES MOTHER GOOSE

edited by

IONA OPIE

illustrated by

ROSEMARY WELLS

WALKER BOOKS
AND SUBSIDIARIES
LONDON · BOSTON · SYDNEY

HERE COMES MOTHER GOOSE

Long ago, when the troubadours still roamed the lanes of Europe, a wise old bird called Mother Goose began to save small fragments of the songs that people most enjoyed. (She was called Frau Gosen in those days.)

As she wandered, she overheard men singing as they worked in the fields, and women singing as they rocked their babies to sleep, and she kept the songs warm under her wings. She listened to children at their play, and to grandads in chimney corners, reciting the sagacious distichs they had learned from *their* grandfathers. She invented rhymes to help babies find out where their eyes and noses are, and rhymes to help older children learn their numbers and the alphabet.

Nonsense verses she liked, and clever riddles. And more than all the others she liked the songs that run in people's heads and make them skip instead of walk, or dance around a room all on their own. This immortal lady has never stopped collecting; from every century she has stashed away the best.

IMPTY 1 DIMPTY 2 TIPSY-TEE 3 OKA-POKA 4 DOMINEE 5

When Mother Goose discovered how much *nicer* children are when fed on nursery rhymes, she published the rhymes in little books and added illustrations. The first, *Tommy Thumb's Pretty Song Book*, 1744, measured but 3 x 1¾ inches, and was adorned with thirty-six miniature engravings. Now, 250 years or so later, we have a book big enough to hide behind in a railway carriage, and as full of colour and revelry as anyone could long for on a grey winter's day. Rosemary Wells has created a host of memorable characters: cosy mother rabbits, cheeky ducklings, resolute and responsible dogs, adventurous cats. A family of guinea pigs act as clowns. They turn cartwheels and stand on their heads (an upside-down guinea pig is called a "pinny gig"). Ten of them, below, persuade us that topsy-turvy and frack-to-bont is the most delightful way to live: their names are

Impty, Dimpty, Tipsy-tee,
Oka-poka, Dominee;
Hocus-pocus, Dominocus,
Om, Pom, and Tosh.

Iona Opie

HOCUS-POCUS

6

DOMINOCUS

7

8

OM

POM

9

TOSH

10

Mabel, Mabel,
strong and able,

Take your elbows
off the table.

6

Contents

One-ery, two-ery, tickery, ten,
Bobs of vinegar, gentlemen.
A bird in the air,
a fish in the sea,
A bonny wee lassie
came singing to me.

Chapter One
1, 2, Buckle My Shoe

Buckle my shoe;

Knock at the door;

Pick up sticks;

Lay them straight;

9 10

A big fat hen.

Mary, Mary, quite contrary,

How does your garden grow?

With silver bells and cockleshells,

And pretty maids all in a row.

Hot cross buns, hot cross buns;
One a penny poker,
Two a penny tongs,
Three a penny fire shovel,
Hot cross buns.

I had a sausage,
a bonny
bonny sausage,
I put it
in the oven
for my tea.

I went down
the cellar,
to get the
salt and pepper,
And the sausage
ran after me.

Bobby Shaftoe's gone to sea,
Silver buckles at his knee;
He'll come back and marry me,
Bonny Bobby Shaftoe.

ld King Cole

Was a merry old soul

And a merry old soul was he;

He called for his pipe

And he called for his bowl

And he called for his fiddlers three.

18

Cross-patch, draw the latch,
Sit by the fire and spin;
Take a cup, and drink it up,
Then call your neighbours in.

I had a little hen
The prettiest ever seen;
She washed up the dishes,
And kept the house clean.

She went to the mill
To fetch me some flour,
And always got home
In less than an hour.

21

Brush hair,

brush,

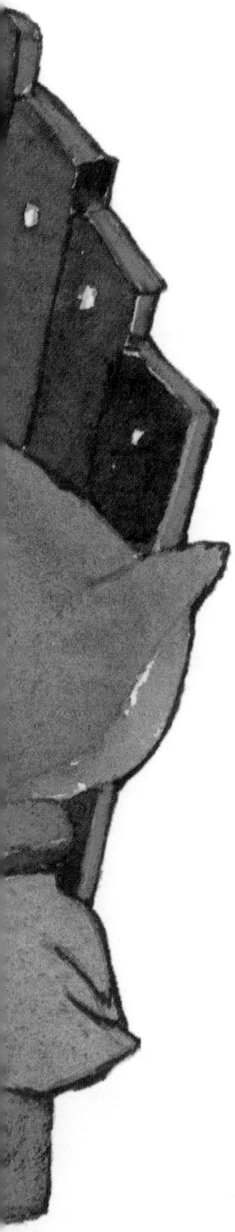

The men are gone
to plough,
If you want to brush
your hair,
Brush your
hair now.

23

Jelly on a plate,
  Jelly on a plate,
Wibble, wobble, wibble, wobble,
Jelly on a plate.

Sausage in a pan,
Sausage in a pan,
Frizzle, frazzle, frizzle, frazzle,
Sausage in a pan.

Baby on the floor,
Baby on the floor,
Pick him up, pick him up,
Baby on the floor.

What are little girls made of, made of?

What are little girls made of?

Frogs and snails and puppy-dogs' tails,

That's what little girls are made of.

What are little boys made of, made of?

What are little boys made of?

Sugar and spice and all things nice,

That's what little boys are made of.

Simple Simon met a pieman,

Going to the fair;

Says Simple Simon to the pieman,

Let me taste your ware.

Says the pieman to Simple Simon,

Show me first your penny;

Says Simple Simon to the pieman,

Indeed, I have not any.

Will you come to my party,
will you come?
Bring your own bread and butter
and a bun;
Mrs Murphy will be there,
Tossing peanuts in the air,
Will you come to my party,
will you come?

RSVP

I asked my mother for fifty cents,

   To see the elephant jump the fence,

He jumped so high,

   He reached the sky,

And didn't come back till the Fourth of July.

Red sky at night,
Shepherd's delight;

Red sky in the morning,
Shepherd's warning.

Chapter Two
Old Mother Hubbard

Old Mother Hubbard

Went to the cupboard,

To fetch her poor dog a bone;

But when she got there

The cupboard was bare

And so the poor dog had none.

She went to the fishmonger's

To buy him some fish;

But when she came back

He was licking the dish.

Chapter Two
Old Mother Hubbard

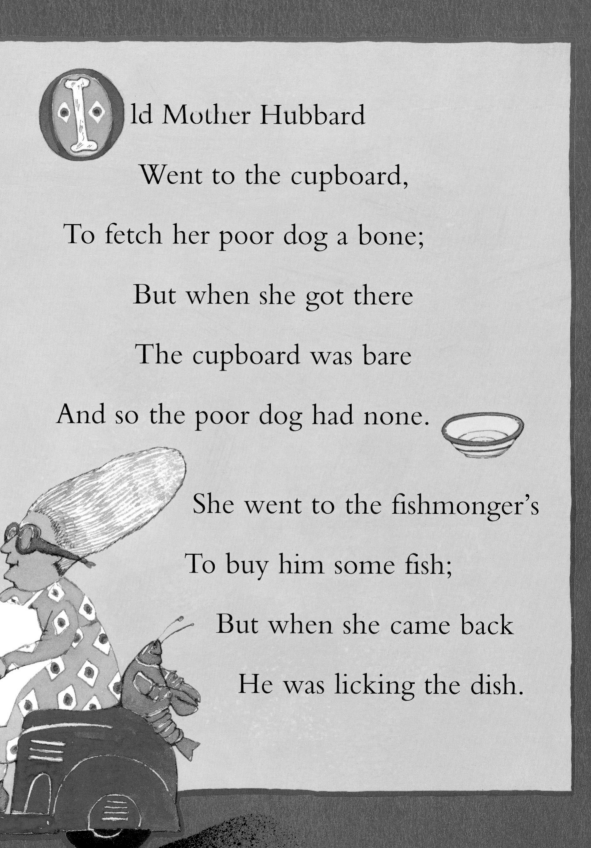

Old Mother Hubbard

Went to the cupboard,

To fetch her poor dog a bone;

But when she got there

The cupboard was bare

And so the poor dog had none.

She went to the fishmonger's

To buy him some fish;

But when she came back

He was licking the dish.

She went to the fruiterer's

To buy him some fruit;

But when she came back

He was playing the flute.

I'm Dusty Bill

From Vinegar Hill,

Never had a bath

And I never will.

Early in the morning at eight o'clock
You can hear the postman's knock;
Up jumps Ella to answer the door,
One letter, two letters, three letters, four!

LAND OF THE MID-DAY MOON

POST CARD

Hello!

Having a wonderful
Wish you were here!

Love,
S. Claus x

CANCELLED

Ella Bunny
1 Whitehall Avenue
Deal 7053

AIR MAIL

REPUBLICA FOOF

AIR

SPIRITUS DENTUS

Miss Ella Bunny
1 Whitehall Ave
Deal 7053

Easter Bunny. Room 41
HOTEL SOCRATES

1ST CLASS

AMBIDEXTROS

AIR MAIL
AIR MAIL

KOPI

Ms. Ella Bunny
1 Whitehall Ave.
Deal, 7053

Ma Goose
Hotel des Palmes
Yanga

URGENT

Miss Ella Bunny
1 Whitehall Ave.
Deal 7053

AIRMAIL
PAR AVION

My Aunt Jane,

She came from France,

To teach to me the polka dance;

First the heel,

And then the toe,

That's the way

The dance should go.

Policeman, policeman,

do your duty,

Here comes Freda the American beauty,

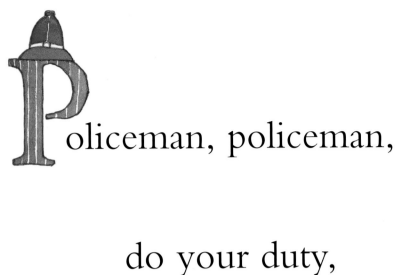

She can wiggle, she can waggle,

She can do the high kicks,

But I bet your bottom dollar

That she can't do the splits.

Here we go round

        the mulberry bush,

    The mulberry bush,

        the mulberry bush;

        Here we go round

        the mulberry bush,

On a cold and frosty morning.

Little Tommy Tucker
Sings for his supper;
What shall we give him?
Brown bread and butter.
How shall he cut it
Without e'er a knife?
How will he be married

Without e'er a wife?

My mother and father are Irish,

We live upon Irish stew;

We bought a fiddle for ninepence,

And that was Irish too.

The wood was dark,
The grass was green,

M y mother said
That I never should

I paid ten shillings
For an old blind horse;

Up comes Sally
With a tambourine;

Play with the pixies
In the wood;

I jumped on his back
And off in a crack,

I went to the river,
I couldn't get across,

Sally tell my mother
That I'm coming right back.

I saw a ship a-sailing,
A-sailing on the sea,
And oh, but it was laden
With pretty things for thee!

The captain was a duck
With a packet on his back,
And when the ship began to move
The captain said, Quack! Quack!

51

The cat's got the measles,
The measles, the measles,
The cat's got the measles,
Whatever shall we do?

We'll send for the doctor,
  The doctor, the doctor,
We'll send for the doctor,
  And he'll know what to do.

Manchester Guardian,

Evening News,

Here comes a cat

In high-heeled shoes.

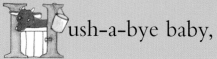ush-a-bye baby,

They're gone to milk,

Lady and milkmaid all in silk,

Lady goes softly, maid goes slow,

Round again,

round again,

round they go.

56

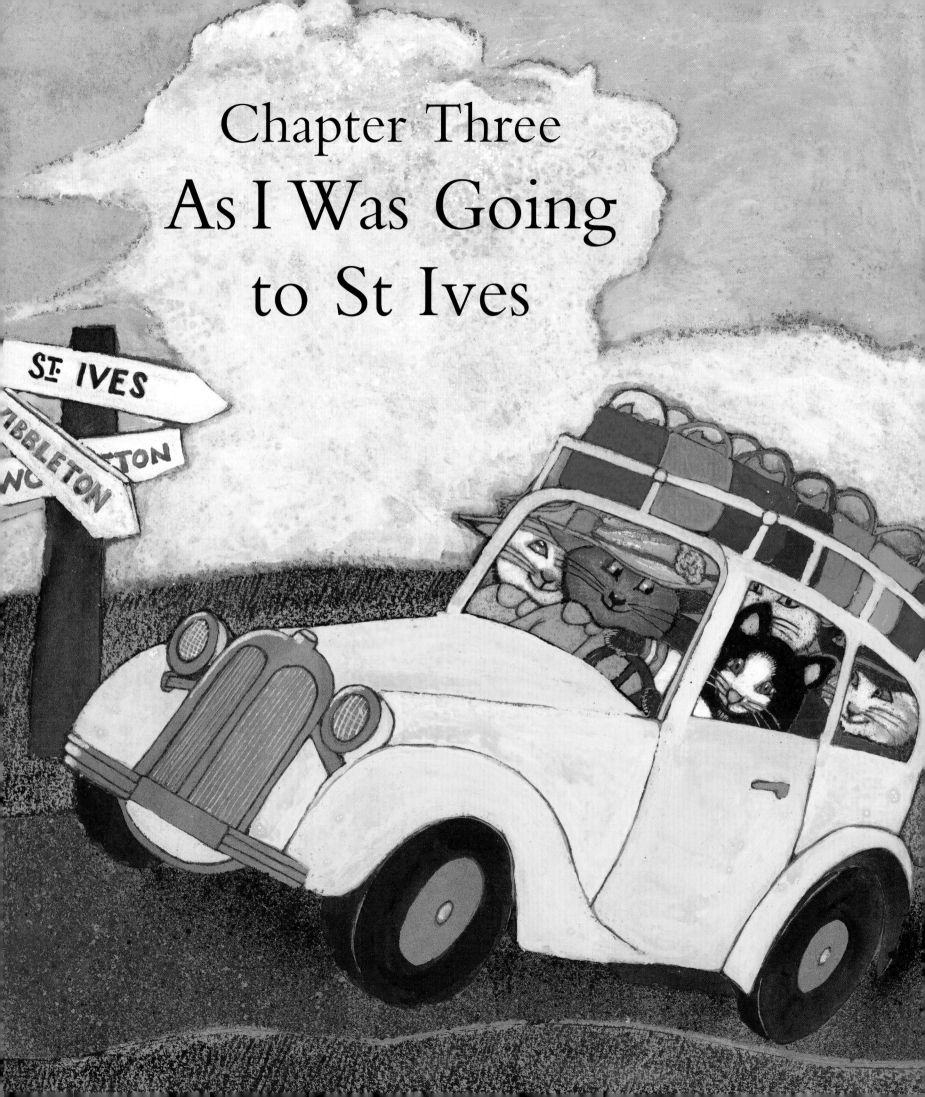

Chapter Three
As I Was Going to St Ives

ST. IVESAs I was going to St Ives,   I met a man

VINEGAR HILL

with seven wives.   Each wife had seven sacks.

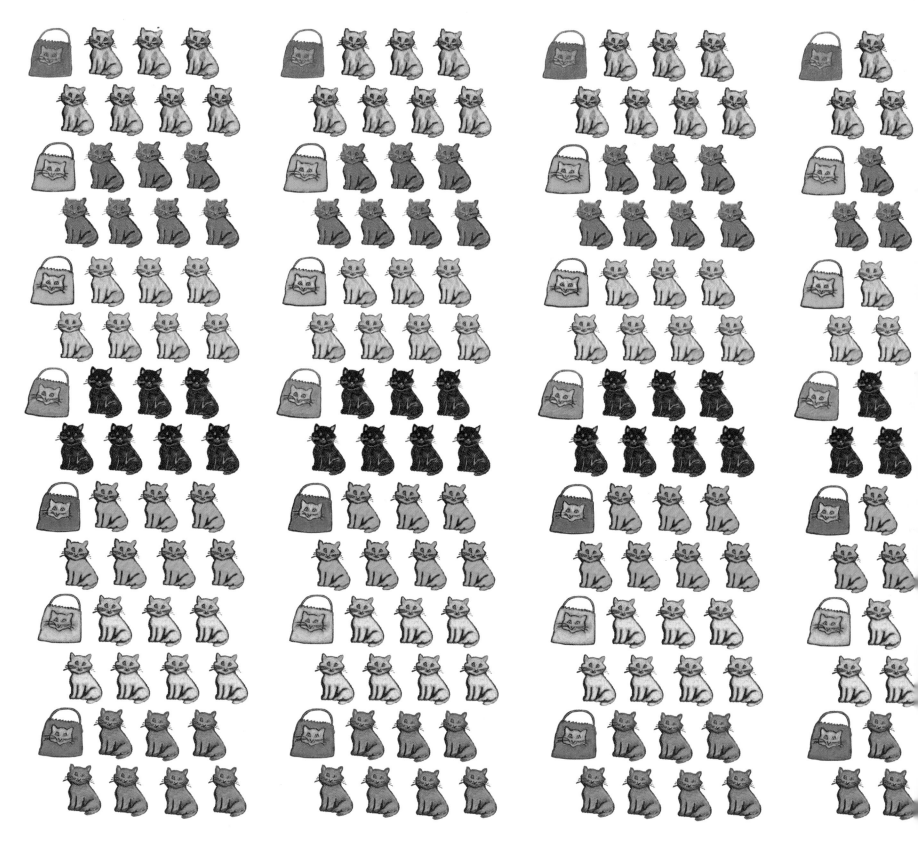

Each sack had seven cats.

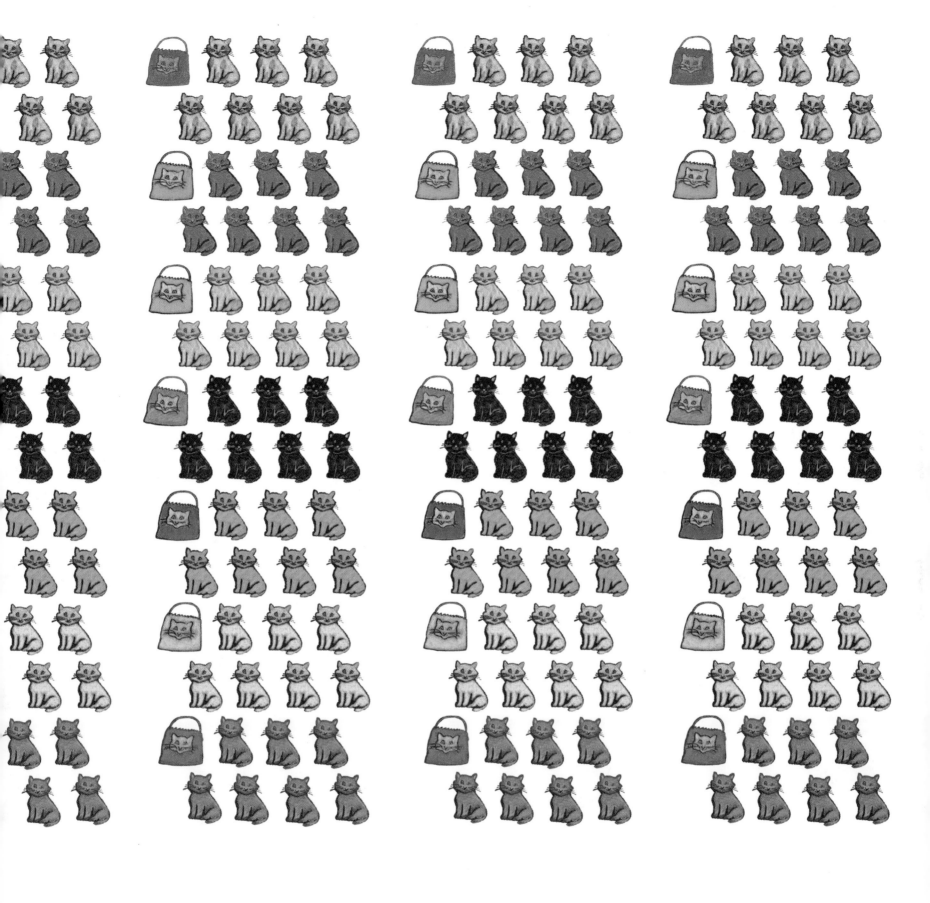

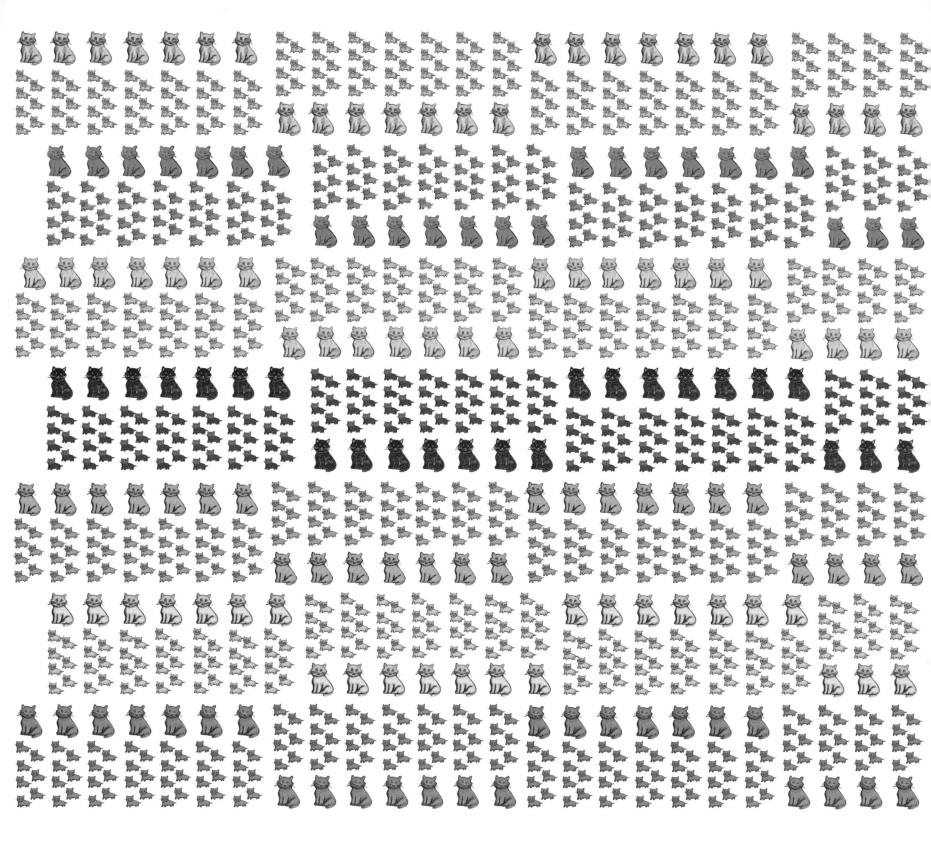

Each cat had seven kits.   Kits, cats, sacks and wives:

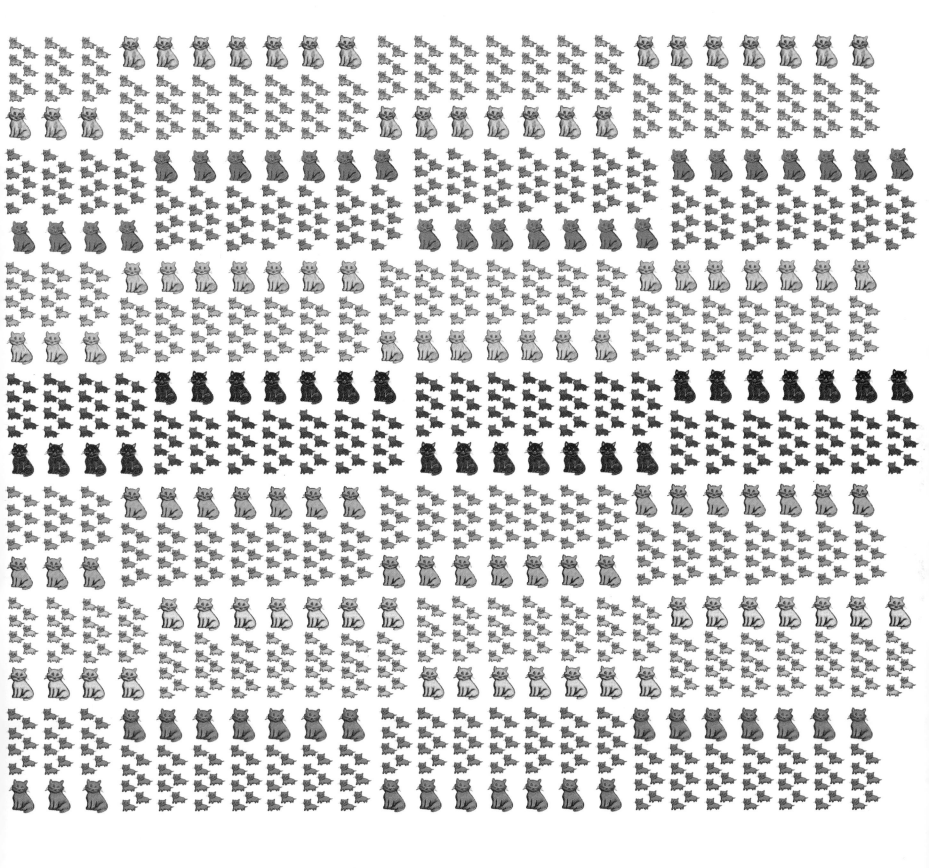

how many were there going to St Ives?

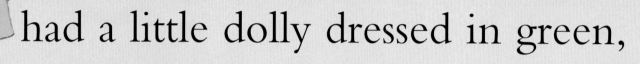 had a little dolly dressed in green,

I didn't like the colour so

 I sent it to the queen;

The queen didn't like it so

I sent it to the king,

 The king said,

Close your eyes and count sixteen.

I am a Girl Guide
dressed in blue,
These are the actions
I must do:
Salute to the king,
Curtsey to the queen,
And turn my back to
the washing-machine.

bowline

square

clove hitch

Donkey, donkey, old and grey,

Open your mouth and gently bray.

Lift your ears and blow your horn

To wake the world this sleepy morn.

I'm a little teapot, short and stout,

Here's my handle,

Here's my spout.

When the tea is ready, hear me shout,

Pick me up and

Pour me out!

71

My ma's a millionaire,

Sky-blue eyes

and curly hair;

She can

play the violin,

Sitting on a biscuit tin.

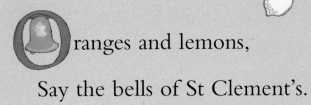ranges and lemons,

Say the bells of St Clement's.

St Clement Danes

St Mary Whitechapel

Two sticks and an apple,

Say the bells at Whitechapel.

Kettles and pans,

Say the bells at St Anne's.

St Anne's Soho

St Martin-in-the-Fields

You owe me five farthings,

Say the bells of St Martin's.

When will you pay me?

Say the bells at Old Bailey.

St Sepulchre Old Bailey

St Leonard's Shoreditch

When I grow rich,

Say the bells at Shoreditch.

Pray when will that be?

Say the bells at Stepney.

St Dunstan Stepney

St Mary-le-Bow, Cheapside

I'm sure I don't know,

Says the great bell at Bow.

Pease porridge hot,

Pease porridge cold,

Pease porridge in the pot,

Nine days old.

le palmier

la cuillère

le chapeau

y'à bon!

PORRIGE
des
POIS
CHAUD!
PORRIGE
des
POIS
FROID!
TOUJOURS
dans le Pot
9
JOURS

Christopher Columbus
was a very great man,
He sailed to America
in an old tin can.

The can was greasy,

And it wasn't very easy,

And the waves grew higher,

and higher,

and higher.

Wake up, baby, day's a-breaking,

Peas in the pot and a hoe-cake baking.

D iddle, diddle, dumpling,

my son John,

Went to bed with his trousers on;

One shoe off,

and one shoe on,

Diddle, diddle, dumpling,

my son John.

winkle, twinkle,

little star,

How I wonder what you are!

Up above the world so high,

Like a diamond in the sky.

Chapter Four
I Danced
with the
Girl

I danced with the girl

With a hole in her stocking,

And her heel kept a-rocking,

And her heel kept a-rocking;

I danced with the girl

With a hole in her stocking,

We danced by the light of the moon.

Bluebells, cockleshells,

    Evie, ivie, over,

Mother's in the kitchen

Doing a bit of stitching,

Baby's in the cradle

Playing with a rattle,

A rickety stick, a walking stick,

One, two, three.

Mademoiselle
she went to the well,
She didn't forget her
soap and towel;
She washed her hands,
she wiped them dry,
She said her prayers,
and jumped up high.

Tinker, tailor,

Soldier, sailor,

Rich man, poor man,

Ploughboy,

Thief.

Peter, Peter, pumpkin eater,

Had a wife and couldn't keep her;

He put her in a pumpkin shell

And there he kept her very well.

90

Sieve my lady's oatmeal, grind my lady's flour,

Put it in a chestnut, let it stand an hour.

My father's a king and my mother's a queen,

My two little sisters are dressed all in green.

Sukey, you shall
be my wife
And I will tell you why:
I have got a little pig,
And you have got a sty;

I have got a
dun cow,
And you can make good cheese;
Sukey, will you marry me?
Say Yes, if you please.

93

The Queen of Hearts
　She made some tarts,
　　All on a summer's day;

94

The Knave of Hearts
He stole the tarts,
And took them clean away.

Down in the valley where the green grass grows,

There's a pretty maiden she grows like a rose;

She grows, she grows, she grows so sweet,

She sings for her true love across the street.

Tommy, Tommy, will you marry me?

Yes, love, yes, love, at half past three.

Ice cakes, spice cakes, all for tea,

We'll have our wedding at half past three.

Ride a cock horse

　To Banbury Cross,

To see what Tommy can buy;

　A penny white loaf,

　A penny white cake,

And a two-penny apple pie.

As I was walking through the City,

Half past eight o'clock at night,

There I met a Spanish lady,

Washing out her clothes at night.

First she rubbed them, then she scrubbed them,

Then she hung them out to dry,

Then she laid her hands upon them

Said: I wish my clothes were dry.

 El Jabón   La Luna   La Camisa

Away down east,
away down west,

Away down Alabama,

The only girl that I love best

Her name is Susianna.

C ome, crow! Go, crow!

   Baby's sleeping sound,

And the wild plums grow in the jungle,

   Only a penny a pound.

Only a penny a pound, Baba,

   Only a penny a pound.

104

There was a man of double deed
Sowed his garden full of seed.
When the seed began to grow,
'Twas like a garden full of snow.

INDEX OF FIRST LINES

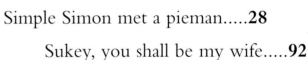

First published 1999 by Walker Books Ltd
87 Vauxhall Walk, London SE11 5HJ

2 4 6 8 10 9 8 7 5 3

This selection © 1999 Iona Opie
Illustrations © 1999 Rosemary Wells

This book has been typeset in M Bembo.

Printed in Hong Kong

British Library Cataloguing in Publication Data
A catalogue record for this book is
available from the British Library.

ISBN 0-7445-5554-X